W9-BLU-176

The Gingerbread Man

Pictures by KAREN LEE SCHMIDT

SCHOLASTIC INC.
New York Toronto London Auckland Sydney

No part of this publication may be reproduced in whole or in part, or stored in a
retrieval system, or transmitted in any form or by any means, electronic, mechanical,
photocopying, recording, or otherwise, without written permission of the publisher.
For information regarding permission, write to Scholastic Inc.,
730 Broadway, New York, NY 10003.

ISBN 0-590-41056-3

Text copyright © 1967 by Scholastic Inc.
Illustrations copyright © 1985 by Karen Schmidt
All rights reserved. Published by Scholastic Inc.

Art direction by Diana Hrisinko
Book design by Emmeline Hsi

70 69   13 14 15 16/0

Printed in the U.S.A.   40

Once upon a time there was
an old man
and an old woman
and a little boy.

One day the old woman said to the little boy,
"I will bake you a gingerbread man."
And she did.

The old woman put the gingerbread man into the pan.
And she put the pan into the oven.

"Now watch the oven,"
said the old woman. "And when you
can smell the gingerbread, call me.

But do NOT open the oven door."

Then the old woman
went to work in the garden
with the old man.

The little boy sat in the kitchen
and watched the oven.
Soon he could smell the gingerbread.

"I want to see if the gingerbread man
looks as good as he smells,"
said the little boy.

And he opened the
oven door.

The gingerbread man hopped out of the pan.
He hopped out of the oven.
He ran across the kitchen
to the open door.
The little boy ran to shut the door,
but the gingerbread man ran faster.

He ran
out of the
door and down
the steps and
into the road.

Then he called out,
"Run, run
as fast as you can.
You can't catch me.
I'm the gingerbread man."

The little boy ran after him.

The old man and the old woman
saw the gingerbread man. And they ran too.
But the gingerbread man ran faster.

And the little boy and the old man
and the old woman had to sit down to rest.

The gingerbread man ran on.
Soon he came to some farmers.

"Where are you going?"
shouted the farmers.

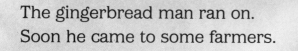

"I have run away from
a little boy
and an old man
and an old woman.
And I can run away from you too,"
said the gingerbread man.

"Oh you can, can you?" said the farmers.
And they dropped their rakes
and ran after him.

Then the gingerbread man called out,
   "Run, run
      as fast as you can.
      You can't catch me.
      I'm the gingerbread man."

The farmers ran fast.
But the gingerbread man ran faster.

And the farmers had to sit down to rest.

The gingerbread man ran on.
Soon he came to a bear.

"Where are you going?" shouted the bear.

"I have run away from
a little boy
and an old man
and an old woman
and three farmers.
And I can run away from you too,"
said the gingerbread man.

"Oh you can, can you?" the bear said.
  And he began to run after the gingerbread man.
  Then the gingerbread man called out,
    "Run, run
      as fast as you can.
      You can't catch me.
      I'm the gingerbread man."

The bear ran fast.
But the gingerbread man ran faster.

And the bear had to sit down to rest.

The gingerbread man ran on.
Soon he came to a wolf.

"Where are you going?" shouted the wolf.

"I have run away from
a little boy
and an old man
and an old woman
and three farmers
and a bear.
And I can run away from you too,"
said the gingerbread man.

"Oh you can, can you?" said the wolf.
And he began to run after the gingerbread man.

Then the gingerbread man called out,
"Run, run
as fast as you can.
You can't catch me.
I'm the gingerbread man."

The wolf ran fast.
But the gingerbread man ran faster.

And the wolf had to sit down to rest.

The gingerbread man ran on.
Soon he came to a fox.

The fox said,
"Where are you going?"

"I have run away from
a little boy
and an old man
and an old woman
and three farmers
and a bear
and a wolf.
And I can run away from you too,"
said the gingerbread man.

The fox said,
"I can't hear you,
gingerbread man.
Come a little closer."

The gingerbread man
stopped running.
He came a little closer
to the fox.

Then he called out,
"I have run away from
a little boy
and an old man
and an old woman
and three farmers
and a bear
and a wolf.
And I can run away from
you too."

"I can't hear you," said the fox.
"Come a little closer."

The gingerbread man came very close to the fox.
Then he shouted, "I have run away from
a little boy
and an old man
and an old woman
and three farmers
and a bear
and a wolf.
And I can run away from
you too."

"Oh you can, can you?"
said the fox.

And snip-snap —
He opened his mouth. And he closed his mouth.

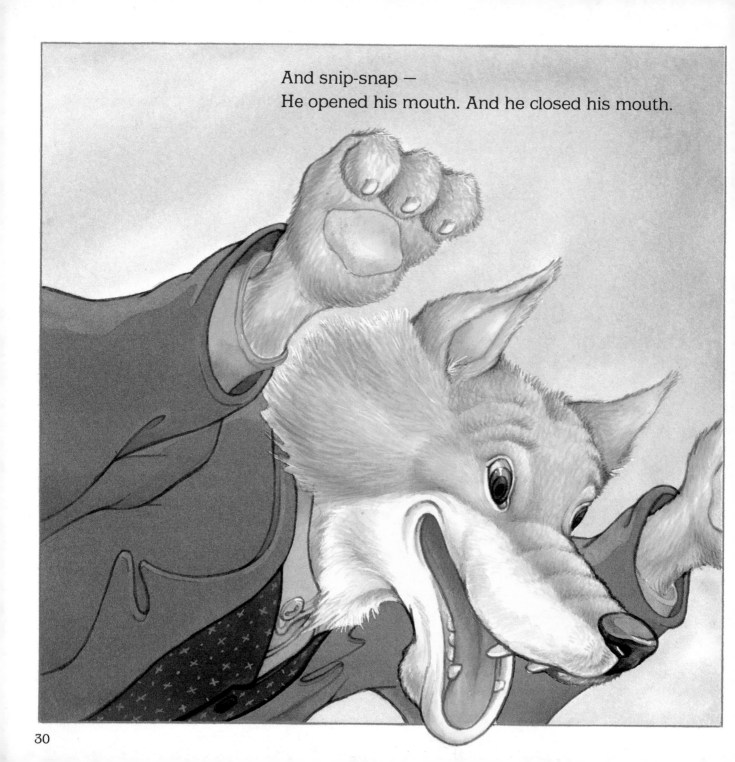

And that was the end of
the gingerbread man!